Studio Fun International
An imprint of Printers Row Publishing Group
A division of Readerlink Distribution Services, LLC
9717 Pacific Heights Blvd, San Diego, CA 92121
www.studiofun.com

© & ™ 2021 Lucasfilm, Ltd.
Adapted by Brooke Vitale

All rights reserved. No part of this publication may be reproduced, distributed, or transmitted in any form or by any means, including photocopying, recording, or other electronic or mechanical methods, without the prior written permission of the publisher, except in the case of brief quotations embodied in critical reviews and certain other noncommercial uses permitted by copyright law.

Printers Row Publishing Group is a division of Readerlink Distribution Services, LLC.
Studio Fun International is a registered trademark of Readerlink Distribution Services, LLC.

All notations of errors or omissions should be addressed to Studio Fun International, Editorial Department, at the above address.

ISBN: 978-0-7944-4769-4
Manufactured, printed, and assembled in Dongguan, China.
Third printing, June 2021. RRD/06/21
25 24 23 22 21   3 4 5 6 7

STAR WARS®

THE
MANDALORIAN

VOLUME 1

ON AN ICY PLANET, A MASKED MAN FOLLOWED A TRACKING FOB. This was the Mandalorian, a famed bounty hunter. It was his job to capture people and things for whoever hired him.

The tracker beeped.

The Mandalorian's next bounty was near.

The tracker led the Mandalorian to a cantina, where he found who he was looking for: a blue-skinned Mythrol man.

The Mythrol tried to bribe the Mandalorian, but the Mandalorian just stared at him.

"I can bring you in warm, or I can bring you in cold," the Mandalorian said at last.

With his Mythrol bounty in tow, the Mandalorian made his way to his ship, the *Razor Crest*.

Suddenly, the ice beneath the Mandalorian's feet began to crack. Mando raced for his ship, dragging the Mythrol with him. But as the ship took off, an icy sea monster called a ravinak rose out of the water.

The ravinak lunged and caught the *Razor Crest* in its jaws.

Snatching a rifle, the Mandalorian leaned out of the ship and jabbed the weapon at the ravinak. Electricity surged through the beast's body. The ravinak loosened its jaw, and the *Razor Crest* flew away.

The Mandalorian took the *Razor Crest* to the planet Nevarro. There, he met Greef Karga, an important man in the Bounty Hunters Guild, to talk about his next job.

Greef offered Mando several bounties, but they were all too small for such a famed hunter.

Greef admitted there was one other job he could offer. It would be dangerous but paid well.

Mando took the job.

The Mandalorian wound his way through town to meet with his mysterious client.

"Greef Karga said you were coming," said the Client, who would not give his real name. "He also said you were expensive."

The Client showed Mando a pouch. Inside was a single bar of beskar. Beskar was a valuable metal used to forge Mandalorian armor. The Client promised that Mando would get even more beskar if he found the bounty.

Mando accepted a tracking fob that he could use to find the bounty's location and left the Client's compound.

Mando followed the tracking fob's signal to the planet Arvala-7. He had not been on the planet long when he was attacked by a blurrg—a big, strong beast. A second blurrg charged the Mandalorian, but before it could join the fight, it fell to the ground, sedated by a dart.

A moment later, an Ugnaught riding a third blurrg appeared.

The Ugnaught introduced himself as Kuiil.

He offered to help the Mandalorian on his mission. There was just one catch: to reach his bounty, Mando first needed to learn how to ride a blurrg.

Once the Mandalorian learned how to ride, he and his blurrg reached the fortress where the bounty was being kept. But a bounty droid named IG-11 had beaten him there.

The fortress's guards began firing on the droid, and IG-11 began firing back.

Mando joined the battle, but he and IG-11 were outnumbered. Soon they were backed into a corner.

They were trapped!

"Manufacturer's protocol dictates I cannot be captured," said the droid. "I must self-destruct."

"Do not self-destruct!" Mando yelled. "Cover me!"

Mando ran for the door to the fortress while the droid continued firing on the guards. Once all the guards were gone, Mando and the droid blew open the door.

Inside, Mando and the droid found what looked like a floating silver oval. Mando touched a button and the top opened.

A small green being looked out at them. It was just a child!

The droid raised its weapon. "The commission was quite specific," it said. "The asset was to be terminated."

Mando was not yet sure who or what this child was, but he was not going to let it die. He fired at the droid, which fell to the ground.

His bounty secure, the Mandalorian left the fortress behind. But as he made his way toward the *Razor Crest*, he was attacked by three lizard-like beings called Trandoshans.

Mando easily fought them off. To his surprise, he found that one of them had a tracking fob. It seemed that he and IG-11 were not the only bounty hunters looking for the Child.

The Mandalorian and the Child returned to the *Razor Crest*, only to find a group of Jawas stripping it for parts. Frustrated and angry, Mando chased after the Jawas' sandcrawler. He climbed aboard, but the Jawas blasted him with electricity, and Mando fell from the sandcrawler, unconscious.

When he awoke, Mando went to see Kuiil.

"My ship has been destroyed," he said. "I'm trapped here."

"Stripped, not destroyed," Kuiil corrected him. Mando could still get back the parts to his ship.

Kuiil took Mando to the Jawas, who agreed to return the parts to the Mandalorian . . . if he would bring them a prized mudhorn egg.

The Mandalorian agreed, and the Jawas took him to the cave of the fearsome mudhorn.

Mando cautiously entered the cave. Inside he saw large bones. He heard a low growl. And then he spotted an enormous eye.

A moment later, Mando was flying through the air. He landed outside the cave. The large, angry mudhorn followed.

Mando tried to fight off the mudhorn, but it was too strong for him. Time and again it knocked him to the ground. Then, just as he could take no more, the Child raised his hand.

The mudhorn rose into the air, unable to move.

Mando took his opportunity. He stabbed the mudhorn, defeating it.

The Mandalorian went into the mudhorn's cave and retrieved the egg. He took it to the Jawas, who happily cut it open to eat the yolk.

With his ship parts returned, Mando set about repairing the *Razor Crest* with Kuiil's help.

Then it was time for Mando to leave. He had a bounty to deliver.

Back on the planet Nevarro, the Mandalorian took the Child to the Client.

The Client gave Mando twenty bars of beskar! "Such a large bounty for such a small package," the Client observed.

As a scientist took the Child away, Mando heard the Child start to cry.

"What are your plans for it?" Mando asked.

But the Client would not answer. "Is it not the Code of the Guild that these events are now forgotten?"

Mando knew the Client was right. He took the beskar and left. He gave the beskar to the Armorer, a fellow Mandalorian who lived in a Mandalorian community.

The Armorer melted down the beskar and forged it into new armor for Mando. With the excess, she forged whistling birds, a rare Mandalorian weapon.

The Mandalorian knew it was time to move on—to secure his next bounty. But he could not stop thinking about the Child's cry. Mando realized he could not leave the Child with the Client.

Mando returned to the Client's compound late that night and rescued the Child. But as he tried to leave, he was stopped by a group of stormtroopers. Mando set down the Child and activated the whistling birds the Armorer had made. The unique weapons took out the stormtroopers with small explosions.

In the nearby public house, all the bounty hunter tracking fobs began to blink. It meant the Child was on the move and there would be a reward for his return.

After the Mandalorian defeated the stormtroopers, he found himself surrounded by Greef's bounty hunters. Each one wanted to claim the Child—and the reward—for their own.

Mando fired at the bounty hunters. The bounty hunters shot back. Blaster fire filled the air.

Suddenly, Mando heard a noise in the sky. Looking up, he saw the rest of the Mandalorians. They had come to help!

"Get out of here. We'll hold them off," one told Mando. "This is the Way."

Mando raced to his ship and took off as the Mandalorians continued to fight.

Mando knew he had to find a safe place to hide with the Child. He decided on Sorgan, a farming planet with no spaceports and no busy cities.

As the *Razor Crest* flew overhead, Mando saw a small fishing village. Children played happily in the water, chasing frogs.

It was the perfect place to lay low.

But laying low wasn't as easy as it seemed. When the Mandalorian entered an eating establishment, he saw a woman watching him suspiciously. The two fought, but neither could get the better of the other, so they gave up.

The woman's name was Cara Dune.

She was a former Rebel and thought Mando was there to collect a bounty on her. "One of us is gonna have to move on, and I was here first," Cara told Mando.

Mando sighed. "Well, looks like this planet is taken," he told the Child.

That evening, two people from Sorgan approached the
Mandalorian. They wanted his help with raiders who were attacking
their village.

When Mando heard that the people lived in a fishing village in the
middle of nowhere, he agreed to help—if they would give him and the
Child a place to stay.

Mando asked Cara Dune to come with him to spy on the raiders. They discovered that the raiders had an AT-ST! The AT-ST was a giant walker once used by the Empire.

Cara knew they would need a plan to fight something as big as an AT-ST. They would turn one of the fishing ponds into a deep hole. When the AT-ST stepped into it, it would fall and be unable to get back up.

For days, the villagers worked to set the trap. Mando and Cara taught them to defend themselves. Finally, it was time.

Cara and Mando lured the AT-ST to the fishing village.

The raiders surged up behind it, firing their weapons. The villagers fired back.

Finally, the AT-ST fell into the water.

Mando raced forward and planted an explosive on the AT-ST. It went off, destroying the walker.

With their AT-ST gone, the raiders fled.

The villagers celebrated. They had won!

The next morning, the Mandalorian watched the Child playing happily with the other children. He asked Omera, a woman in the village, if she would take care of the Child if Mando left him there. She agreed.

But as Mando prepared to leave, Cara Dune found and killed a bounty hunter. The bounty hunter had been there looking for the Child.

Mando realized that it was too dangerous to leave the Child behind. They had to stay together.

Mando and the Child took off once again in the *Razor Crest*. Sometime later, another ship fired on them. An alarm went off, and the *Razor Crest* lost power.

Mando needed to land—and fast!

Mando touched down on a planet called Tatooine. After hiding the Child on board, he walked off the *Razor Crest*. In the hangar, he found a mechanic named Peli Motto.

Peli examined the ship. "Look at that. This is a mess," she said. "That's gonna set you back."

"I'll get you your money," Mando said.

Before Peli Motto could get to work on the *Razor Crest*, its ramp lowered and the Child walked out.

Peli picked up the Child. "Did that bounty hunter leave you all alone in that big, nasty ship?" she asked.

Despite herself, Peli felt drawn to the Child. She decided to look after him until Mando returned.

Across town, Mando entered a cantina looking for a job. But it seemed there was no work to be found.

Just then, a man called out to Mando. "If you're looking for work, have a seat, my friend."

The man's name was Toro Calican. He was a bounty hunter too. Toro was tracking an assassin by the name of Fennec Shand. Fennec was well-known for being as smart as she was deadly.

Mando knew it was a dangerous job, but he had no choice. He needed money to fix his ship.

Soon the two were on their way across the desert to find Fennec.

From a high ridge in the desert, Fennec watched the two bounty hunters approach.

As they drew closer, she fired at them, but the blast bounced off the Mandalorian's beskar armor.

Mando needed a plan. He decided to wait Fennec out.

As night fell, Mando and Toro snuck up on the assassin. They captured her, but Fennec was as smart as her reputation said. When Mando left to get transportation, she convinced Toro that bringing in Mando would be worth a lot more money than she would.

Toro was smart too. He shot Fennec and then raced back to town. The Mandalorian found him a short time later—with Peli Motto and the Child. Toro wanted to bring Mando in and was using Peli and the Child as hostages.

Mando knew he had no choice. He fired at Toro, who fell to the ground.

Mando took Toro's credits and handed them to Peli. She had fixed the *Razor Crest*. It was time for Mando and the Child to move on.

Mando piloted the ship to a small space station. There, he found an old ally: Ranzar Malk.

Ran needed help with a job, and Mando needed money.

Ran introduced Mando to his crew: Mayfeld, Burg, Xi'an, and Zero. They would be working together to free one of their teammates from a New Republic prison ship.

The crew easily broke into the prison ship. They looked in cell after cell, but they could not find the prisoner they were seeking. They would need to go to the control room.

But when they got there, they found a problem: a human guard. The ship was supposed to be staffed only by droids!

The guard activated a tracker, alerting the New Republic to trouble on board.

The crew had to act fast. They only had twenty minutes before the
New Republic's attack team arrived and blew up the ship.

They quickly made their way to their teammate's cell, fighting
security droids on the way. There, they found Qin, Xi'an's brother.

The crew released Qin, but they were not so generous to the
Mandalorian.

They shoved him into Qin's cell and locked him inside.

Mando lured over a security droid and used it to open his cell. Then he raced back to his ship and flew off, leaving everyone but Qin behind. He needed Qin so he could get the reward.

Mando delivered Qin to Ranzar on the space station.

But as Mando flew away, Qin found the tracker from the prison ship in his pocket. The Mandalorian had planted it on him!

The New Republic attack ships followed the tracker—and blew up Ran's space station.

Mando knew he could not keep running. The only way to keep the
Child safe for good was to get rid of the Client. He made a deal with
Greef Karga, then asked Cara Dune for help. She agreed, and together
they traveled to Arvala-7.

When they arrived, Mando found Kuiil with IG-11, the droid that
had been programmed to kill the Child. Kuiil had reprogrammed IG-11
to be a nurse droid! IG-11 vowed to protect the Child.

Mando explained that he needed Kuiil to care for the Child while the others dealt with the Client. Kuiil agreed, and the group flew to Nevarro.

Greef and his men were waiting when they arrived.

As the group traveled together to meet the Client, they were attacked by fierce beasts.

Mando and his friends defeated the creatures, but Greef was badly injured in the battle.

As Cara and Mando tended to Greef, the Child approached. He put a tiny hand on Greef, and with great concentration, he began to heal the man.

Cara, Greef, and Kuiil watched, stunned. They realized that the Mandalorian was right: the Child had to be protected at all costs.

The next morning, two of Greef's men tried to turn on them, but Greef killed them first. "The plan was to kill you and take the kid," he confessed to Mando. "But after what happened last night, I couldn't go through with it."

The Mandalorian decided to send Kuiil and the Child back to the *Razor Crest*, where IG-11 waited. Then Mando, Greef, and Cara left to meet the Client.

They made the Client think they had the Child with them. He was eager to see the Child again. But just as he was about to discover that the Child was not there, the room exploded with blaster fire and the Client fell to the ground.

The Client's superior, Moff Gideon, had arrived with an army of stormtroopers.

Gideon offered Mando an ultimatum: give him the Child or die.

Elsewhere, Moff Gideon's scout troopers had gotten to Kuiil before he could reach the *Razor Crest*. He had been killed, and the Child had been taken.

But IG-11 had been true to its new programming. The droid had gotten the Child back, protecting him at any cost.

Now it was taking the Child to Mando. The droid and the Child zoomed into town on a speeder bike.

At last, IG-11 arrived with the Child. Mando, Cara, and Greef raced outside while IG-11 fought the stormtroopers. They tried to help IG-11, but Mando was injured in the battle.

They retreated back inside the building. IG-11 set to work opening a grate that led to the sewers—and freedom.

But before they could escape, Moff Gideon's incinerator trooper entered with a flamethrower.

Fire filled the room.

The Child stepped forward. Raising his hand, he forced the flames out of the room—and back onto the trooper.

The way was clear, but Mando was too injured to move. While the others went on, he and IG- 11 stayed behind. IG-11 removed Mando's helmet and treated his wounds. Once Mando could walk, he and IG-11 followed the others into the sewers.

Soon the group found their way to the Armorer. All around her lay pieces of Mandalorian armor. The other Mandalorians had been hunted by the Empire for helping Mando.

The Armorer asked to see the Child.

"By Creed, it is in your care," the Armorer told Mando. "Until it is of age, or reunited with its own kind, you are as its father."

The Armorer gave the Mandalorian a jetpack and a special signet on his armor. Then she pointed the group toward the lava river.

They followed the Armorer's directions and found a boat waiting on the lava river. The group climbed aboard and made their way downstream.

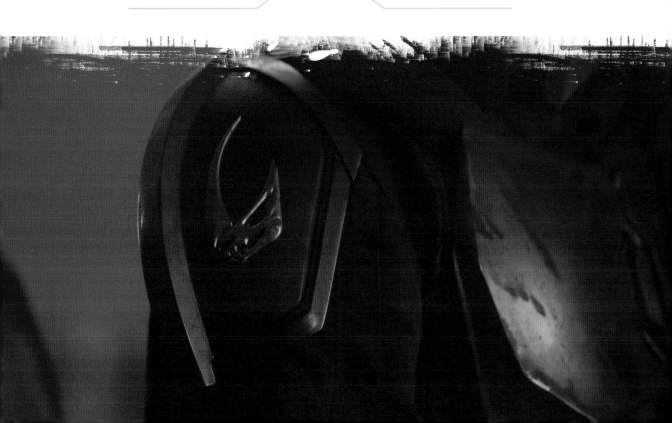

Just outside the sewer tunnel, Mando saw an army of stormtroopers waiting for them. There was no way out.

IG-11 stepped forward. "I will eliminate the enemy," it said.

The droid walked into the lava river and made its way toward the waiting stormtroopers.

"Manufacturer's protocol dictates I cannot be captured," IG-11 said when it reached the stormtroopers. "I must be destroyed."

IG-11 activated its self-destruct function and blew itself up—along with the stormtroopers.

As the boat moved into the sunlight, the Mandalorian saw that all the stormtroopers had been defeated. IG-11 had saved them.

Suddenly, there was a loud noise overhead. It was Moff Gideon in an Imperial TIE fighter. He started firing on Mando and his friends.

Firing up his jetpack, Mando flew into the air. He landed on top of the TIE fighter and planted an explosive charge.

The charge blew, and the TIE spiraled out of control, crashing to the ground.

With Moff Gideon and the Client gone, the Child was at last safe. But Mando's journey with him was only just beginning. He needed to find the Child's family and return him home.

"Take care of this little one," Cara said.

"Or maybe," Greef added, "it'll take care of you."

Mando nodded and activated his jetpack. It was time to go. He and the Child shot into the air.

Not far away, Jawas gathered around the fallen TIE fighter to strip it for parts. Suddenly, a blade cut through the side of the ship.

Out stepped Moff Gideon, wielding the Darksaber, a legendary black lightsaber. Gideon looked out over the remains of his ship.

Mando was gone, but Gideon would find him. . . .

On board the *Razor Crest*, Mando looked at the Child,
who was holding something in his hand.

It was a necklace—the Mandalorian's necklace. Mando
had given it to Cara when he was injured and thought he
would not survive.

"I didn't think I'd see this again," Mando said. Then,
giving it back to the Child, he added, "Why don't you
hang on to that?"

And with that, Mando lifted off. He had a galaxy to
explore and a Child to return to his family.